CAROLINDA CLATTER!

MORDICAI GERSTEIN

ROARING BROOK PRESS

NEW MILFORD, CONNECTICUT

For
Risa Faye Amelia Harris-Gerstein
With all my Love

TRA
LA
TRA LA-LA
TRA LA
TRA TRA-LA-LA

Once there was a
lonely giant who fell
in love with the
moon.

He was the very last
giant, and there was
no one else large
enough for him
to love.

"Dear Moon," he sang.
"Come dance and
marry me.
We'll have a lovely
family of little giants
and pretty planets—
maybe even a comet
or two!"

But the moon shone
coldly and silently
and said nothing.

For five
thousand years
the giant sang and
danced for her.
He begged and
pleaded with her.

But the moon
sailed across the sky,
waxing and waning,
waning and waxing,
and ignored him.

The giant lay down, looked up at her, and for ten thousand years
he raged and wailed, he moaned and wept.

SOB!
SOB! SOB!
MOAN
WAIL!
SOB
HOWL!
SOB
AAARRGH!
HOWL!
BOO-HOO!
WAH!
SOB!
WAH!
OOOOOH!
WAH!
MOAN!
BOO-HOO
BOO-HOO!
WAH!
WAH!
SOB
SOB!
WAIL!
HOWL!
SOB

Finally, he fell asleep. Even as he slept, he wept.
Over a hundred years, grass grew all over him.

After ten thousand years, his eyes became two ponds.
His tears became two waterfalls.

His beard and the hair on his head became forests.

All kinds of animals came to live in them.

After a hundred thousand years, people came.

They said, "This mountain looks just like a sleeping giant.
We must be quiet and careful not to wake him."

So they walked on tiptoe and whispered. And they quietly built
a town right on the spot that looked like the giant's belly.

The town was called Pupickton.

Over hundreds and hundreds and hundreds of years, the legend grew—about how the mountain was a sleeping giant hopelessly in love with the moon, and if he was ever wakened his rage and grief would destroy the town. And so, just in case the legend was true, no one ever made any noise. Pupickton was a very quiet town.

Babies didn't cry and children were afraid to scream and yell because everyone said, "Shhhh! You'll wake the giant." No one laughed. No one wept. You couldn't tell if they were happy or sad. No one sang. There was no music. No one even sneezed. The animals were quiet too—no moos or barks. No twitters or chirps. The only sounds were whispers and the purring of cats.

Then, one night, Carolinda Clatter was born.

She was born NOISY.

"Shhh," whispered her parents.

Carolinda tried to be quiet.

"You'll wake the giant."

But the bigger she grew, the louder she got.
She cried, she laughed, and she sang all the time.

"Shhhhhhhhhhhh!" the whole town whispered.

"You'll wake the giant!"

But Carolinda just banged on pots and pans for good measure.
The people of Pupickton hid under their beds and lived in fear.
"Any minute now," they whispered, "you'll wake the giant!"
"I can't help it!" she shouted. "I love NOISE!"

Hearing Carolinda, birds began to chirp. Cows began to moo.
Dogs barked and howled. Cats yowled.

Sure enough, one morning, the ground began to tremble.
The people heard a low rumble. . . .
The rumble became a grumble . . .

. . . and the grumble became a tumble of words so low and loud and old and rusty that everyone knew it could be only one thing. And they were terrified.

"Carolinda," the people whispered.

"Now you've done it. You woke the giant.

You must go and tell him to go back to sleep."

"Oh, dear!" said Carolinda. "Must I?"

"Yes," they whispered. "You must!"

Trembling, Carolinda went up the hill called Giant's Chest and
into a tangled forest called Giant's Beard, up to The Mouth,
a huge, dark cave full of moans and sighs.

Singing made her feel a *little* less frightened. But just a little.

Waterfalls ran down both sides of a peak called The Nose
from ponds called The Eyes.
"Excuse me, Mr. Giant, sir. I am Carolinda Clatter. It was
I who woke you."

"Is it you," rumbled the voice, "who sings the beautiful songs
and makes the beautiful music?"

"It's just noise," said Carolinda. "But it's what I love to do."

"It's MUSIC!" said the giant. "I haven't heard music for thousands
and thousands of years! It makes me HAPPY! It makes me want
to get up and dance with the moon! I'm in love with her, you know,
but she won't have me. . . ."

"Mr. Giant, sir . . ." said Carolinda.

"My name is Hugene," said the giant. "And I want to DANCE!"

The giant tried to rise and the whole world shook.

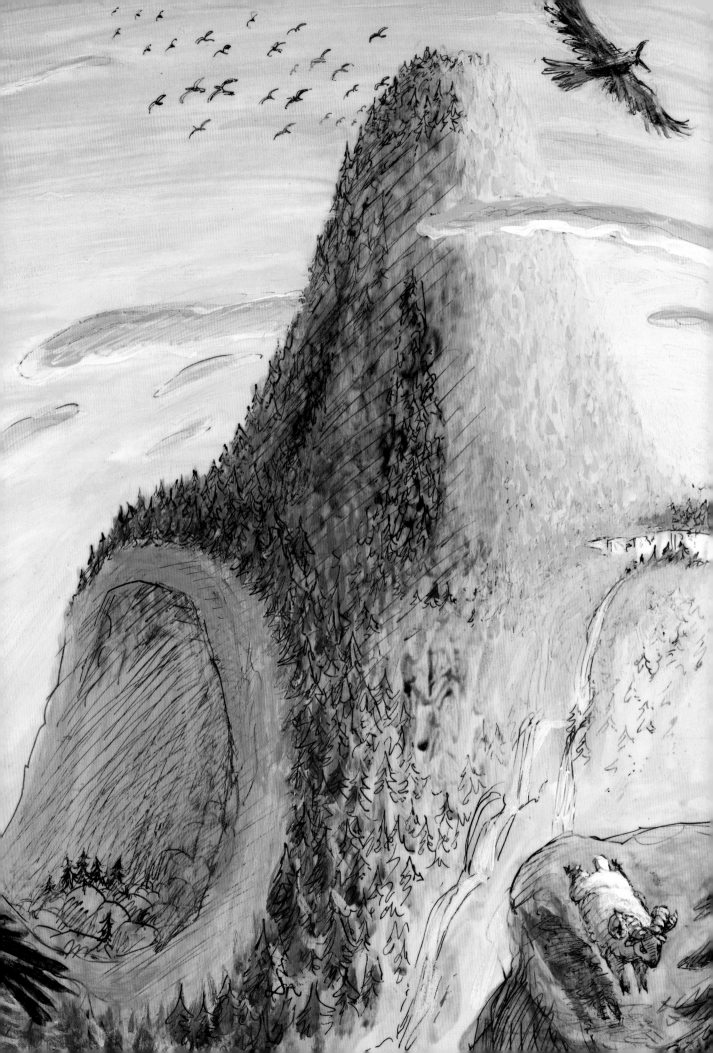

"Mr. Hugene Giant, sir," said Carolinda. "Many animals, birds, and people are living on you. They need you and love you. You are a mountain now, and mountains do not dance."

The giant was silent for a long moment.
"Am I really a mountain?" he asked. "Am I truly loved?"

"Yes," said Carolinda. "And when the moon is full, she shines on you and makes you all silvery."

"Do you think," asked the giant, "that maybe now . . . she likes me?"

"I believe that she loves you," said Carolinda.

"Ahhhhh. . . ," sighed the giant. "I almost gave up hope. I will lie here and adore her. And I will be a great mountain. But Carolinda please, every evening, would you sing me a song? A sweet, happy song. A soft, soothing song?"

Carolinda sang a lullaby.

The giant yawned an enormous, mountainous yawn, and fell into a deep, deep sleep, never to wake again.

LA LA LA LULLA
LULULA LULLU BY
LALA LA LULALA
LULA LALA LULLABY
LALA LA LULLABY

Carolinda went back to the town and told all that had happened.

"Are we safe now?" everyone whispered.

"Yes!" said Carolinda.

There was a long, deep, sigh of relief. Then there were giggles.

Then there was laughter and shouting, cheering and applause.
"HOORAY FOR CAROLINDA!"
Then Carolinda taught them all to sing.

Every evening they went up the mountain and sang a lullaby
to the giant. Then they laughed and danced into the night.

Carolinda grew up, and she and all her children, and their children's children's children, were famous for their singing. Now visitors come from all over the world to hear the music of the people of Pupickton. Their music makes everyone laugh and cry and cheer. It makes people happy.

Even the giant of the mountain, sleeping on and on,
happily dreams that he's dancing with the moon.

Published by Roaring Brook Press
Roaring Brook Press is a division of
Holtzbrinck Publishing Holdings Limited Partnership
143 West Street, New Milford, Connecticut 06776

Distributed in Canada by H.B. Fenn and Company, Ltd.

Library of Congress Cataloging-in-Publication Data
Gerstein, Mordicai.
  Carolinda Clatter! / Mordicai Gerstein.— 1st ed.
        p. cm.
  Summary: The excessively quiet town of Pupickton and the sleeping lovesick giant
upon which it was built, are both awakened by the joyful noise of a little girl's songs.
  [1. Fairy tales. 2. Giants—Fiction. 3. Moon—Fiction. 4. Noise—Fiction.
  5. Lullabies—Fiction.]   I. Title.
  PZ8.G34C 2005
  [E]—dc22   2004024258

ISBN: 1-59643-063-X

Roaring Brook Press books are available for special promotions and premiums.
For details, contact: Director of Special Markets, Holtzbrinck Publishers.

First edition September 2005
Book design by Filomena Tuosto
Printed in the United States of America

10 9 8 7 6 5 4 3 2 1